Frank raced out in front, running up the hill to Phil's house. The road was so steep his legs hurt. When they turned the corner, they noticed Phil was outside. His face was bright red. His mom and dad were right next to him. Frank and Joe hadn't seen him this upset since he'd spilled water on his computer keyboard.

"What's wrong?" Frank yelled.

Phil was pulling at his dark brown hair. He looked like he might cry. That's when they noticed the garage behind him. It was completely empty.

"Someone must've stolen it!" Phil said. He was out of breath, like he'd just run a mile. His mom put her hand on his back to calm him down. "Our robot is gone!"

CATCH UP ON ALL THE HARDY BOYS® SECRET FILES

THE HARDY BOYS®

SECRET FILES #11

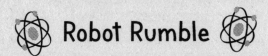

Robot Rumble

BY **FRANKLIN W. DIXON**

ILLUSTRATED BY **SCOTT BURROUGHS**

ALADDIN ▪ NEW YORK LONDON TORONTO SYDNEY NEW DELHI

ALADDIN

An imprint of Simon & Schuster Children's Publishing Division

1230 Avenue of the Americas, New York, NY 10020

First Aladdin paperback edition April 2013

Text copyright © 2013 by Simon & Schuster, Inc.

Illustrations copyright © 2013 by Scott Burroughs

All rights reserved, including the right of reproduction in whole or in part in any form.

ALADDIN is a trademark of Simon & Schuster, Inc., and related logo is a registered trademark of Simon & Schuster, Inc.

THE HARDY BOYS is a registered trademark of Simon & Schuster, Inc.

For information about special discounts for bulk purchases, please contact Simon & Schuster Special Sales at 1-866-506-1949 or business@simonandschuster.com.

The Simon & Schuster Speakers Bureau can bring authors to your live event. For more information or to book an event contact the Simon & Schuster Speakers Bureau at 1-866-248-3049 or visit our website at www.simonspeakers.com.

The text of this book was set in Garamond.

Manufactured in the United States of America 0615 OFF

10 9 8 7 6 5 4 3 2

Library of Congress Control Number 2012939454

ISBN 978-1-4424-5367-8

ISBN 978-1-4424-5368-5 (eBook)

CONTENTS

Science Fair Countdown

Joe moved around the cramped garage. He squeezed past cardboard boxes, a pile of rusty rakes and shovels, and the old kitchen table his mom had refused to throw out. The Hardys had two garages side by side. His father parked his car in one, and the other was the place the family stored all the things they didn't use— like his dad's collection of posters from old police movies.

Joe grabbed the metal sled propped against the

wall. "Look!" he yelled over his shoulder. "What do you think, Frank? I bet we could use this for finishing the robot's back."

A voice crackled from outside the garage door. "This is Agent Hardy requesting Agent Hardy's assistance. Come in?" When Joe turned back, he noticed a small walkie-talkie sitting on the grass outside the garage door. Frank's voice sounded again. "Come in? Come in?"

Joe took the sled out of the garage, careful not to step on any of the old knitting magazines his mom was saving. He dropped the sled on the grass and grabbed the walkie-talkie, pressing the button on the side. "Heard you loud and clear, Frank. Over and out."

"Requesting assistance at the back exit—" Frank said, his voice interrupted by static.

Joe ran to the back door just in time to open it. Frank strode through, carrying a whole stack of flat silver pans. A few rolls of tinfoil were stacked on top of the pans. "Look what Mom gave me. They have to be good for something, right? Then we can see if Phil can use these old walkie-talkies to make the robot speak."

"This is perfect," Joe said. He held up the sled. "I was thinking we could use this to cover its back, where some of the wires stick out. Now we just need to find that silver paint we were looking for. . . ."

Frank set the pans and foil on the lawn. They had enough to finish up the robot tonight. "I can't believe the science fair is tomorrow. Those judges would be crazy not to pick us!"

It was Friday afternoon, and at noon the next day was the Bayport Science Fair. Frank and Joe had spent the last three weeks working with one of their best friends, Phil Cohen, on their project.

Phil had been obsessed with electronics ever since they were in first grade. He always had the latest computer or video game. Other kids from Bayport spent their afternoons playing baseball or camping out by the school jungle gym. But Phil took apart computers or helped his mom fix the broken appliances in his house. One time Frank and Joe came over after he had dissected his father's old treadmill, just to see how it worked.

With Phil on their team this year, the boys decided to make a robot. They'd finished up most of the robot's insides, and they had already hooked up the parts that made its arms move. Plus, they had a cool feature. Frank had found a busted stereo in the attic, and after Phil fixed it and installed it, if you pushed a button, music came out of the robot's ears! For the first time, they actually had a *real* chance of winning the fair.

"I don't know what Cissy is bringing to the fair this year," Frank said, "but I sure hope we can compete with it."

Cissy Zermeño, one of their friends from their baseball team, won the science fair nearly every year. The year before, she'd won by finding out how plants respond to music. The year before that, she did an experiment where she used a plastic tennis ball container to speak underwater. Sometimes it seemed like no one could top Cissy's projects. The judges, who worked at the Natural History Museum in the city, were always impressed.

"I heard Adam is making another volcano," Joe said. "It's probably the same one he used last year."

Frank shook his head. Normally, he'd feel bad for someone who brought the same project to the science fair every year, but Adam Ackerman was different. He was the biggest bully in Bayport. Kids flinched every time they passed him in the halls. In the last two months he'd put a toad in their friend Callie's book bag and had threatened to punch Chet Morton just because Chet "looked at him funny." And he was constantly shoving Phil whenever he saw him. Adam spent so much time in the principal's office that people joked he had a special seat reserved for him.

"Callie won't tell anyone what her project is, and Melissa and Todd are keeping theirs a secret too," Frank added.

"I can't wait to see what Phil did," Joe said. They were storing the robot a few blocks away in Phil's garage. He'd found a used blender at a yard sale and had taken the motor out. Tonight, after they got the last of their supplies, they were going to help him put it in the robot's neck. With one push of a button, it would make the robot's head spin! "Who else could make a robot that plays music? Or whose head goes around in circles?"

"Or one that can move its arms like this?" Frank stood perfectly straight, imitating the five-foot-tall robot. He bent his arms at right angles and shuffled around. The whole time he kept his body completely stiff.

"I am the smartest robot on earth," Joe said in a mechanical voice. He walked around the same way Frank did, each movement stiff. "I will fight you with my laser-beam eyes."

They kept walking around like that. "Robots will take over the world!" Frank yelled. He raised both his arms in the air. "Robots unite!"

Joe karate-chopped Frank's shoulder with one flat hand. "I'm a warrior robot from Mars!" he yelled. "I will ruin you!"

They moved across the yard in slow motion and pretended to battle. The whole time Frank's face never changed. It was perfectly still, like it was made of metal.

"Am I interrupting?" someone with a familiar voice called out. The boys turned to see their dad, Mr. Hardy, standing on the back porch. He was holding a silver paint can. "Were you robots looking for this?"

The boys froze in place, still pretending to be robots. Mr. Hardy didn't miss a beat. He set the paint can down on the steps and jumped into position, his back straight as he shuffled past them. "I am father robot from Mars!" he said. "I will eat your brains!"

The boys ran from him. He chased them around the yard, then tackled them in one of his big hugs. They laughed so hard their sides hurt. "We need our brains, Dad!" Frank yelled as he wriggled free of Mr. Hardy's grip. "We have the science fair tomorrow!"

2

Meet Mr. Roboto

A few hours later Frank and Joe were at Phil's house. After many weeks of work, their robot was almost done. "It's still not as good as I want it to be," Phil said, pressing the tinfoil around the robot's neck. He stood on a chair as he did it, using the last of the foil to cover the motor he had put in. "The head doesn't spin around fast enough, and I can't get him to really walk the way I wanted him to. The feet aren't locked on tight enough either. . . ."

"It's fantastic, Phil—really, it is," Frank said. He painted the robot's side with the silver paint their father had given them. "Don't sweat the small stuff—that's what our mom always says." He glanced down at Joe, who was working on the robot's feet—two remote-control cars that shot out from the body. They'd known Phil since kindergarten, and he'd always been a perfectionist. Even if he made a rocket ship that blasted to the moon, he would think it could've been better. They always tried to remind him how amazing his inventions were.

"We just have to wait for the paint to dry," Joe said. "Then it'll be done!" They'd used a trash can for the robot's body, with an old radio for the head. Phil had finished the last of the electronics. There was no way they wouldn't win. The robot looked like he'd stepped out of a Hollywood movie!

Phil kneeled down. He wedged the foot in, but it came loose again. "This won't fit right," he said. He tried to lock the car into the robot's body, but it was still wobbly. "Maybe we should use something else—like bike tires?"

"We might just have to leave it that way." Joe shrugged. "But I don't think they'll notice after this. . . ." He pressed two buttons on the robot's front and the head spun around. Music blasted from the robot's ears.

"I've never seen anything so cool!" Frank said. He couldn't stop smiling.

A loud barking came from down the street. Phil's house was at the top of a big hill. They could see all of Bayport from there. Wilmer Mack, an older man who was Phil's neighbor, was walking up the road with his dog, Lucy. "Whoa, slow down, girl!" he yelled. "It's not going to hurt you!" The dog broke free and ran at the robot. She stood in front of it, baring her teeth. She wouldn't stop barking.

Mr. Mack walked up to the garage door and put his hands on his hips. "Well, I'll be!" he said. "That's the neatest robot I've ever seen." As he spoke he grabbed Lucy's collar to pull her back.

"We built it for the science fair tomorrow," Phil explained.

Frank clasped his hands together. "We want to win, but we have some tough competition. Cissy always has the coolest projects. She usually comes in first."

Mr. Mack smiled. He was about to say something, but Lucy caught sight of a squirrel in his front yard. She started toward it, yanking Mr. Mack away. "I'd say good luck," he yelled over his shoulder, "but you guys don't need it!"

More hopeful than ever, Frank and Joe watched

Mr. Mack go. Tomorrow, at the Bayport Science
Fair, they might finally take first place.

The next morning Frank and Joe practically ran
to Phil's house. They kept imagining the
judges' faces when they saw the robot.
They would *ooh* and *ahh* as the robot's
head spun. They'd watch its arms
move and how it rolled

forward and backward on the remote-control cars. They had to love it. The robot was incredible. Even Mr. Mack had said so! They had worked on the robot after dinner the night before, putting the walkie-talkies in so they could make the robot speak. How could they not get a ribbon this year?

As they ran up the big hill they saw Adam Ackerman coming down it. He was holding his project, but it was covered in a sheet. It looked like a papier-mâché volcano was hidden underneath. "Hi, Adam!" Frank called out quickly. They didn't want to ignore him, but they didn't want to stop to talk either. Sometimes it seemed like Adam had nothing nice to say.

"See you later at the fair!" Joe called over his shoulder. "Good luck!"

Adam looked down at the project beneath the sheet and scowled. "Whatever," he said. "I have something better than anything anyone's ever seen. Get ready to lose!"

Frank and Joe shared a look. They doubted Adam had come up with anything besides a volcano. The year before, he'd used baking soda, vinegar, and some food coloring to make it spew blue lava. He thought that made it a completely different project from the year before that.

"I think we have a real chance," Joe whispered. "Even if Phil was nervous about it, his parents were so impressed." Mr. and Mrs. Cohen had looked at the robot last night after they were done. Frank and Joe had eaten dinner at Phil's house, and Phil's parents couldn't stop talking about it. Mrs. Cohen loved the music best, and Mr. Cohen loved the way its arms moved.

Frank raced out in front, running up the hill to

Phil's house. The road was so steep his legs hurt. When they turned the corner, they noticed Phil was outside. His face was bright red. His mom and dad were right next to him. Frank and Joe hadn't seen him this upset since he'd spilled water on his computer keyboard.

"What's wrong?" Frank yelled.

Phil was pulling at his dark brown hair. He looked like he might cry. That's when they noticed the garage behind him. It was completely empty.

"Someone must've stolen it!" Phil said. He was out of breath, like he'd just run a mile. His mom put her hand on his back to calm him down. "Our robot is gone!"

3

Off to the Fair!

I left the garage door open last night so the paint would dry," Phil explained. "I went to bed around ten o'clock, and when I woke up this morning it was gone. We looked everywhere. Someone must've taken it. It didn't just disappear!" The boys followed Phil through the school lobby. After searching everywhere for the robot, they'd come to the gymnasium. There were only fifteen minutes before the science fair would begin.

"I hope Principal Butler can help," Frank said.

"We just need some time to figure this out."

The front entrance to the gymnasium was decorated with colorful balloons. A giant banner hung over the door. BAYPORT SCIENCE FAIR, it read. Joe tried to stay calm as they pushed inside, without their project. The tables were set up in front of the bleachers. People wandered about, looking at the different projects. Each project looked more impressive than the one before.

Cissy stood beside a giant life cycle of a butterfly. She made each stage out of wire and papier-mâché, showing how the insect grew in its cocoon. Ellie, a freckle-faced girl with blond hair, was their teammate on the Bandits. She'd made a poster titled "Why Is the Sky Blue?" with colorful pictures and diagrams. Chet tested how plants grew under different-colored lights. Iola, his younger sister, had a glass aquarium filled with hermit crabs. There, at the last table, was Adam Ackerman with his latest volcano. This one spit out green lava. He looked more miserable than ever.

"Look at what Cissy did!" Joe whispered to his brother. "Or Chet!"

But Frank didn't respond. He kept his eyes on Principal Butler. She was standing under the basketball hoop with three other adults. Frank could tell by their clipboards that they were the judges. He recognized a woman with a gray streak in her hair from the year before.

"Principal Butler!" Frank called out. "Can we speak with you?"

Before she could say anything, Phil jumped in. When he got nervous or excited about something, he spoke really fast. "Someone stole our project!" he said. "We're sorry, but we don't have it. We may have to forfeit the fair this year."

"Unless you can give us some time," Joe said. "We just need to figure out what happened."

Principal
Butler glanced
at the three
judges. They
looked more
serious than the
boys remem-
bered them. One
man, the head of
the planetarium,
had a long

black mustache that curled up a little at the ends.

"I'm sorry to hear that," Principal Butler said. "I'd love to help, but the science fair begins in fifteen minutes." She pointed to the clock on the wall.

"We need more time than that," Joe explained. "We've been building this robot for weeks. And this morning, when Phil went to get it from his garage, it was gone."

"I don't know what happened," Phil said. He was so nervous his hands were shaking. "It was like it just disappeared."

The woman with the gray streak in her hair looked at them over her tiny glasses. "That is quite the problem. I wish we had more time, but I'm afraid we don't. We have to start the judging on time. . . ."

"We just need a little more time," Frank said.

"Please? Maybe we could be judged last. . . ."

Principal Butler glanced sideways at the judges. "One minute," she said quickly. They huddled together, whispering. Joe and Frank could've sworn they heard them say something about proof. If proof was what they wanted—proof was what they would get.

After a few moments Principal Butler turned back to them. "All right. You'll be judged last. They have to leave at five o'clock, though. So you'll have to be back here before the scoring at quarter to five with your project to be entered into the fair. Is that clear?"

"Crystal," Frank said. He turned and started toward the door.

"I don't know if we have enough time. What are we going to do?" Phil asked.

Frank pulled out a notebook from his pocket. Joe handed him a pen. The Hardy boys were good at building robots. But they were even better at solving mysteries. Frank's notebook was bent and worn from being carried in his pocket all the time. It held the record of every crime they'd ever investigated. "We'll figure it out," he said. "But first we have to go back to the scene of the crime to gather evidence."

"We better hurry," Joe said, racing past the tables of projects. He pointed to the clock that hung above the doors. It was nearly twelve o'clock. They had to be back in the gymnasium, with Mr. Roboto, by four forty-five. "Time is running out!"

4

The Six *W*s of Solving Crimes

Joe inspected the floor of the garage. Right by the door there were a few pieces of tinfoil, some screws, and chips of silver paint. "This is all that's here," he said. "Whoever took him didn't leave much behind."

Frank and Phil searched the rest of the garage, but there were no other signs of Mr. Roboto. Frank inspected the pieces in Joe's hand. "Those came from his foot," he said. "Especially those screws. Phil used them to connect the remote-control cars."

"Those were the exact ones!" Phil said. Since they'd left the auditorium he'd been talking non-stop, wondering if it could've been someone he knew, or if it was kids from another school.

Joe copied down the evidence in his notebook, writing *foil, screws, and paint from robot's feet. Found inside the garage door.* Frank and Joe's dad had worked for years as a private investigator with the Bayport police department. Growing up, they'd spent so much time watching him solve cases. They learned about detective work. Their father taught them how to gather clues and narrow down the list of suspects. The first step, after you surveyed the crime scene for evidence, was writing down the six *W*s—Who, What, Where, When, Why, and How.

Joe flipped the page and scribbled *What* across the top, then *Mr. Roboto* beneath it. "Mr. Roboto disappeared from Phil Cohen's garage," he said. "The robot was approximately five feet tall. He was silver. His body was made from a trash can. He had a stereo for a head and a walkie-talkie at his waist, and his arms moved."

"Why did I leave the door open?" Phil cried. He sat on the front curb and sighed. "Of course someone took him!"

"It's not your fault," Frank said. "We're just trying to be as specific as possible." That was one

of the other things their father had taught them. Many times, the clues were in the details.

Joe continued scribbling in his book. "He was on wheels. He had two remote-control cars for his feet. His head spun at the push of a button, and he had lightbulbs for his eyes."

"Don't forget the sled on his back," Phil said.

Once they were done with the description of Mr. Roboto, Joe turned the page. "Now we need to know when it happened," he said. "What do you think, Phil?"

Phil put his head in his hands. "I left Mr. Roboto in the garage around nine, right after you guys left. Then I was in my room for a while. I read some comic books before I went to sleep around ten."

"So the last time anyone saw Mr. Roboto was at nine o'clock?" Frank asked.

Phil nodded. "Yeah. My parents came inside with me, and they went to bed too."

"Did you hear anything strange in the middle of the night?" Joe asked. If Phil had heard a noise or seen anything suspicious from his window, it could've been a clue. Maybe it would help them figure out when Mr. Roboto was taken.

"Maybe some kids playing around," he said. "Maybe a few cars that drove by. Lucy next door was barking, but she always barks. My mom went into the garage this morning at ten fifteen and the robot was gone."

Joe wrote *between 9 p.m. and 10:15 a.m.* in his notebook. On the following page he printed *Where*. "The Where is easy: 825 Chesterfield Street. Phil's house."

"Right out of my garage!" Phil said. His cheeks were bright red, the way they always looked when he was upset.

"Now for the tricky part," Joe said. "Why?" He wrote it down in his notebook, right under *Where*.

They knew this was always the hardest part of the mystery to figure out. Their dad used to call it the criminal's "motive." Why would anyone want to take Mr. Roboto? They sat there in silence, trying to think of as many reasons as possible.

"They wanted him for themselves," Phil said sadly. "I can't blame them."

Frank scratched his head. "Maybe they thought we were going to win the science fair and they didn't want us to. Maybe we were their competition."

Joe wrote both reasons down. They sat outside Phil's house, thinking of more. As the list went on, Joe scribbled them all in his notebook.

- Someone wants the supplies we used to make Mr. Roboto.
- Another student is playing a prank on us.
- Adam took the robot because he is mad about his project.

- It was an accident—someone took the robot without knowing.

- Mr. Roboto wanted to explore Bayport.

Joe knew the last one was unlikely, but he loved thinking Mr. Roboto was off somewhere on his own. "Who would do this, though?" he asked.

Phil took the notebook from his hands. There was only one name in it—Adam's. "He's never liked me. Ever since we were in first grade, he's been giving me a hard time," he said.

"I don't know . . . ," Frank said. He glanced at Joe. Adam Ackerman was usually a suspect in Bayport mysteries. He didn't like many of the kids at school, and many of the kids didn't like him. But Frank and Joe knew from solving other cases that that didn't mean he was the culprit. "Just because Adam was angry about his project doesn't mean he would steal ours."

"I still don't trust him!" Phil said. "Didn't you say you saw him in my neighborhood right before Mr. Roboto went missing? Maybe it was one of his friends."

"He's right," Joe said. "Even if Adam didn't do it, he might've seen something. He was probably walking past Phil's house right before Phil and his parents found out the robot was missing."

Frank started down the street, heading back to school. Adam was still at the science fair. "Don't worry, Phil. We're going to sort this out," he said. Then he turned to his brother. "Come on, Joe! We have our first suspect to question!"

5

The Usual Suspect

After searching the science fair for Adam, they'd found him outside by the school bleachers.

Adam saw them coming from across the school track. He leaned against the bleachers. He was with his friend Scott, a red-haired kid who lived three houses down from Phil. "Let me guess," Adam said. "You want to blame me for your missing project. Well, I didn't do it!" He frowned. "Besides, I just got disqualified. I guess you can't enter a volcano every year, even if the lava is different."

"Sorry about that," Frank said, not sounding sorry at all. "We just want to talk to you," Frank said. "We did see you leaving the neighborhood this morning."

"That's because I slept over at Scott's house!" Adam said. He crossed his arms. He stepped forward so he was just a foot away from Frank.

Joe looked at Scott, who was sticking a wad of bubble gum under the metal bench. "Is that right?"

"Yeah," Scott said. "He came over yesterday after school, then left when he went to the science fair. He was with me the whole time. He never went near Phil's house."

Joe wrote the word *alibi* in his notebook. His father had used it before. It meant that a suspect had been seen somewhere else when the crime happened. If Adam was at Scott's house from Friday afternoon until Saturday morning, he wouldn't have had time to take the robot from Phil. "Did you see anything when you passed Phil's house this morning?" Joe asked.

"No," Adam said. "I didn't see anything weird. Just an empty garage." He was getting more annoyed as he spoke. He paced back and forth in front of them, his arms crossed over his chest.

"So if the garage was empty when Adam

passed," Frank added, "the robot was probably taken long before Phil went outside. What time was that, Adam?"

Adam let out a sigh. "I'm not answering any more of your questions!" he yelled. "Anyone with two eyes can see it was Puck Craven." He pointed across the track to the edge of the woods. Puck, a pale boy with wild black hair, was standing near the trees. Every time Frank and Joe saw him, he was alone. He walked alone in the halls and sat alone in the cafeteria. He always played arcade games alone at Fun World.

Joe rubbed his eyes as if he couldn't believe what he'd seen. "Is he playing with what I think he's playing with?" he asked. The boys started toward him. Puck held a remote control in his hands. The silver car zipped around the grass. Even from far away they could tell it was one of the same ones they'd used for the robot's feet.

"Puck!" Frank called out across the field. "Where did you get that?"

Puck looked up and his face went white. He picked up the toy car and ran into the woods, dropping the remote. Joe and Frank got across the field just in time to see him disappear behind the trees.

6

The Chase Is On

Puck! Wait!" Joe called after him. But Puck kept going. Frank raced out front, jumping over rocks and fallen tree branches. They darted through the woods, trying to keep their eyes on Puck. Puck sprinted though the trees to where the woods ended and the neighborhood began. He turned right and the boys followed.

Frank could barely breathe, he was running so fast. Puck held the car underneath his arm and turned left, down a narrow street. He passed a few houses before noticing the sign up ahead: DEAD END. Puck kept running, but the street turned into a small court. A bunch of kids were drawing with chalk on the sidewalk. They looked up as he slowed down. He knew he was trapped.

"We just want to talk to you," Frank said. He was nearly out of breath. He stopped a few feet away from Puck and rested his hands on his knees.

Joe studied Puck's face. He looked scared more than anything else.

He held the car in his arms, hugging it to his chest. "Where did you get that car?" Joe asked.

Puck looked around. Then he set the car on the ground and kicked it toward them. "You can have it! Just leave me alone." He turned and walked down the street, trying to get away from them.

Frank followed after him. "We aren't going to get you in trouble! We just want to know where the rest of the robot is," he said. "Please? We just want to enter the project in the science fair. We need all of it—not just one foot!"

Puck spun around. He was in the same black T-shirt he always wore, with an exclamation point on the front. "What robot?" he said. "I don't know what you're talking about. . . ."

Joe picked up the car. It was definitely the one they'd used to make Mr. Roboto. The silver paint was scratched off in places. "Where did you get this, then?"

Puck grabbed the car from Joe and gave it a kick. "Some guy gave it to me."

"Who?" Frank asked.

Puck shrugged. "I was on my way to the park this morning, and this older man brought it up to me. He asked me if it was mine. It just looked so cool, I said that it was. . . ."

Frank and Joe looked at each other. What was a man doing with their robot? "What did he look like?" Joe asked.

Puck stared at the ground. "I don't know. He was wearing a blue sweater. And he had white hair and glasses."

Joe looked at the evidence in his hand. The silver car was pretty beaten up. One of the plastic headlights was broken, and there were scratch marks on its side. But on the front, by the hood, there were a few small dents. "Do these look like bite marks to you?" he asked Frank.

Frank inspected the car. "Yeah . . . like a dog bit down right here."

Joe smiled. They were getting closer. He could feel it! "I only know one man with white hair who owns a dog," he said.

"Thanks, Puck!" Frank yelled as they ran back toward Phil's house.

Puck watched them go. "What? Where are you going? I didn't do anything!"

Frank tucked the car under his arm like a football. "You helped us," he laughed. "We're going to find Mr. Mack!"

7

The Furry Bandit

Why would Mr. Mack want anything to do with our robot?" Phil asked as he, Frank, and Joe walked up the large hill. They looked at the town below. Fun World was just around the corner, and the ice cream shop was two blocks over. They could even see the gymnasium where the science fair was being held.

"It was probably an accident," Frank said. "Or

maybe whoever did it left the remote-control car behind."

They could see Mr. Mack's blue house up ahead. He had a large porch with a swing out front, and tons of plants. Joe looked at his watch. "I hope Mr. Mack has it," he said. "It's nearly three already. If we don't find Mr. Roboto soon, we won't be able to enter the science fair. All that work for nothing!"

"We could enter again next year," Phil said, as if that could make them feel better. "Maybe next year's robot will be even more impressive."

When they got to Mr. Mack's house, he wasn't there. They looked at the empty porch. The windows were dark. There was no sign of him.

"Now what?" Joe asked.

Frank held one finger to his ear. "Listen!"

The boys were quiet for a moment. They could hear a whistling sound coming from somewhere behind the house. Frank laced his fingers together the way his dad had shown him how to do. "Want a lift?" he asked, nodding to the low wooden fence.

Joe stepped onto the footrest, and Frank lifted him up. It was easy to see over the fence when he was a few feet taller! Joe immediately saw Mr. Mack. He was hunched over his vegetable garden, pulling some of the carrots from the ground. "Mr. Mack!" Joe called out. "We need your help!"

Mr. Mack looked up. Lucy, his big yellow dog, darted around the side of the house and started barking again. "Oh shush, Lucy!" he called as he stood up. He took off his gardening gloves and unlocked the fence. "You've been barking all night. Give it a rest, will you?"

"Mr. Mack, we need your help," Frank said. He held up the silver car. "Do you know anything about this?"

"Where'd you find that?" Mr. Mack asked. "I thought that belonged to that boy. He was so convincing. He told me he'd lost the car ages ago. He looked so relieved that I'd found it. I think his name was Paul . . . or Parker?"

"Puck Craven," Phil said. "He had it, but this was from *our* robot. Mr. Roboto is still missing."

Mr. Mack slapped his hand to his forehead.

"I should've known that was from your robot. How silly of me!"

"Where did you find it?" Joe asked. "The robot went missing sometime last night, and no one's seen it since. If we don't find it soon, we won't be able to enter the science fair."

Mr. Mack shook his head. "Last night Lucy got out. She was barking like crazy. I came outside and she had that car in her mouth. The remote was in the bushes. I figured she just found it somewhere. When I asked that boy this morning, he acted like it was his!"

Frank looked at the car, then at the street. There were no other signs of the robot. "What time did that happen?"

Mr. Mack scratched his head. "I think it was around ten o'clock . . . but it could have been a bit later."

"Do you remember if the robot was still in the garage when you went outside?" Joe asked.

Mr. Mack shook his head. "I don't. . . ."

Phil paced back and forth. "If Lucy had the car, that means she was in my garage at some point last night. Maybe something happened," he said.

"But Lucy didn't do it," Joe said. "She's just a dog!"

Mr. Mack pet the dog on the head. "I'm so sorry," he said. "She was using that car as her chew toy! You know dogs, they get into everything. . . ."

Frank headed next door to Phil's house. "Thanks for the help, Mr. Mack," he said as he left. "I think we just need to have another look."

Phil and Joe followed behind him. The garage door was still open. They searched through it again, looking for any clues they may have missed.

"So Lucy was here last night," Frank said. "But why?"

"Maybe she caught someone stealing it," Phil said.

"Or maybe she had something to do with how it disappeared," Joe added.

Frank walked outside, looking at the street. He stared at the hill and the long row of houses in front of them. "Maybe," he said. He tried to figure it out, but the more he thought about it the less it made sense. Lucy was just a dog. She couldn't make a five-foot-tall robot disappear. Wherever it was, wouldn't it be obvious? "It's like Mr. Roboto just vanished. . . ."

Joe looked at his watch again. "We're running out of time," he said. "If Lucy didn't do it, then who did?"

8

A Second Look

Joe and Frank stood in the garage, exactly where the robot used to be. Their dad had told them detectives sometimes missed clues the first time they went to the scene, so it was a good idea to come back a second time. They scanned the road, hoping to see something they hadn't noticed before. Across the street, Mrs. Delilah was watering her roses. The house beside hers was dark. A few little children played a few yards over. They laughed as they ran around in circles.

"Mr. Roboto was standing right here just yesterday," Joe said. "Just yesterday we put on his wheels, connected the cars, hooked up that—"

"Wait!" Frank said. He turned to Joe. "What did you just say?"

"We connected the cars. . . ."

"No," Frank cried, "before that!"

"We put on his wheels?" He said it like it was a question.

Then he nodded. Joe could tell when Frank was onto something. He knew just what it was. . . . "Right!" he added. "Mr. Roboto was on wheels. He had two sets—the ones Phil installed to keep him steady, and his remote-control feet. Whoever took him wouldn't have picked him up—they would've rolled him somewhere."

"Guys," Phil said, "it's getting late. Maybe we should just tell Principal Butler we'll enter the science fair next year?"

Joe scanned the front of Phil's house. He knew what Frank was getting at. If someone had rolled Mr. Roboto out of the garage, there would still be tracks. Very specific tracks. He looked at the dirt driveway, which was scattered with gravel. There were two long, curving lines that led out into the street. They were about a foot apart, and one was much larger than the other. "Look!" he cried. "These look like they came from the tires Phil put on the back of the robot. And this side had wider tracks—"

"Because it still had the remote-control car on it," Frank said. "But if the person wheeled the robot out, where did they wheel it to? And when did Lucy catch them?"

Phil looked more nervous than ever. His cheeks were bright red, the way they always got when he was upset. "The robot wasn't that great anyway," he said. "Maybe it's not worth all the trouble."

For the first time all day Frank noticed how strange Phil had been acting. While Frank and Joe were trying to find Mr. Roboto, it seemed like Phil had already given up. And now he was saying the robot he'd worked on *wasn't that great*? Was it possible he'd had something to do with the robot's disappearance? But why would he get rid of a robot he'd helped make?

Frank followed the tracks, which led to an area

right behind the garbage cans. Ripped pieces of tinfoil sat beside them. "So sometime after nine o'clock someone moved Mr. Roboto out of the garage. Maybe Lucy caught them and ran away with part of the robot. Or . . . maybe she discovered the robot here, behind the trash cans."

"Why would anyone move Mr. Roboto into the trash?" Joe asked.

Frank looked to Phil. Phil's face was deep red.

"Guys . . . I have something to tell you," Phil said. He let out a deep breath. "This is all my fault. Last night I came out to make some finishing touches to the project. I was trying to fix some of the mechanics that weren't working perfectly. I just got so frustrated . . . I pushed the robot into the trash. I just gave up. I was so mad that I wasn't able to get him to work the way I wanted him to. I knew we'd never win the fair with him. You said it yourself, Frank—the competition is so tough this year. Cissy always wins."

"But we had a chance," Frank said. "We did. Because of you, Phil—because of the invention you helped us make."

Joe looked at his friend. He'd never seen Phil so upset. Even though part of him was angry about what had happened, he knew Phil felt terrible about what he'd done. Phil had never thought the robot was good enough, and he was so afraid to lose. "We were just happy we were working on the project with you," Joe said. "Who cares if we didn't win this time? We always lose to Cissy anyway!"

Phil stared at the ground. "I knew I made a mistake. I ran out of the house this morning and the robot was already gone. I'm so sorry. This is all my fault—I've ruined everything."

Just then there was the sound of squeaking tires. The boys turned in time to see the giant garbage truck pass by the bottom of the hill. Black bags were piled high in the back. "Maybe not," Frank said. "We can still get him back. . . ."

Joe took off down the hill, waving his hands in the air. The truck didn't stop. He kept yelling after it. "Stop!" he cried. "You have our robot!"

9

Mystery Man

Please, please," Phil repeated. "Please let the truck have him."

The boys ran as fast as they could. The truck kept going. Smoke rose up from a pipe on top of its hood, and the smell of garbage filled the air. "Oh no!" Joe joked, trying to make Phil feel better. "Mr. Roboto is going to stink!"

When the truck reached the corner, it finally pulled over. It stopped right outside the Grahams' house. The neighbors' house was painted bright red with yellow shutters—everyone always pointed at it as they drove by. "Wait!" Frank yelled. He was nearly out of breath. "We need your help!"

The engine turned off. Two men stepped out of the truck in green jumpsuits. One was tall and thin, with furry black eyebrows. They looked like caterpillars crawling over his forehead. The other was bald with glasses. "What can we help you kids with?" the one with the furry eyebrows said. The name on his uniform said BILL.

"Have you seen a robot?" Phil asked. He reached up high with one hand. "About this tall. He's silver, with a stereo for a head. He has a remote-control foot and arms that move."

The bald man smiled. "Oh yes!" he laughed. "Hard to forget a robot. Don't see those every day. He was sitting a few streets over, by some garbage cans."

Joe let out a deep breath. He turned and looked

at where the man was pointing. It was the exact same spot on the curb where Phil had left him. "We need him back," Joe explained. "He's our science fair experiment. And if we don't get there soon and show him to the judges, all that work will have been for nothing!"

Frank walked toward the truck. He covered his face with his shirt, trying not to let the smell bother him. He didn't want to go searching through piles of garbage to find Mr. Roboto, but sometimes detective work was messy. He reached out his hands, about to climb onto the back of the truck.

"Not so fast, young man!" Bill called. "Your robot's not in there!"

Phil's mouth dropped open. "Then where is he?"

The bald man put his hands on his hips. "We went by that house this morning. It's one of the first stops on our route," he explained. "The robot was lying behind the trash cans."

"We were about to throw him into the back of the truck when a man drove by," Bill said. "He couldn't believe someone would throw the robot away."

Phil rubbed his forehead. "It was a mistake. I made a really bad mistake."

Bill shrugged. "We didn't know that. So this man got out of his car and looked at the robot, and he said he had the perfect place for him."

"Where?" Joe asked.

Bill shook his head. "He didn't say."

Frank scratched his head. "What did the man look like?" he asked. Their father had told them all about questioning witnesses. You had to ask simple questions and let them do all the talking. Mr. Hardy told them to pay attention to everything the witnesses said.

Joe pulled out his notebook as the bald man started talking. "He was short, and had a mustache," he said slowly. "I think . . ."

"He was no shorter than me," Bill said. Joe stared up at the witness. He was nearly six feet tall. Those were two very different descriptions!

"He was, too, short," the other man said. "And blond, maybe."

"Definitely not blond," Bill said. "He had brown hair and no mustache. No beard, either. Trust me." He poked his chest with his thumb.

Joe looked at his watch. They had less than an hour to figure out who this mystery man was, and two witnesses who couldn't agree. What could be worse? "Is there anything you both can agree on? How old was he?"

The bald man rubbed his chin. "Hmmm . . . I'm not sure. I'm bad with ages."

Frank raised his arm in the air. "I got it!" he yelled. "What color car was the man driving?"

"Red," the men said at the same time.

"Are you sure?" Phil asked. He narrowed his eyes at them. He looked more confused than he had all day. Maybe these witnesses weren't the best Joe or Frank had ever met, but they were their only lead. That's what Mr. Hardy called a really good clue—it was a good "lead."

"Positive," Bill said. He pointed down the street. "He went that way."

The bald man nodded. "Yup. Red car, driving

north on Main Street. Hope that helps, kids."

They climbed back into their truck and drove away.

Joe didn't know many people in Bayport who drove a red car. There was Harriet Lynn, the piano teacher who drove a tiny red car. "It couldn't have been Harriet," he said. "They seemed pretty certain it was a man."

"There's Mr. and Mrs. Huntly," Frank added. "But they both wear glasses. And they're over eighty years old. I really don't think they'd want a robot."

"Maybe," Joe said. "You never know."

Just then Phil covered his mouth with his hand. "I think I know!" he yelled. "Doesn't Mr. Fun drive a red car?"

Joe and Frank looked at each other. Phil was right. Mr. Fun, the owner of the Fun World arcade, drove a red car. "And Fun World is right around the corner on Main Street."

Phil shrugged. "What do you think? Could it be him?"

Joe looked back at the notes he'd written down.

short

nearly six feet tall

blond with a mustache

brown hair with no mustache

red car

None of them made sense. Except for the last one. Joe glanced at his watch. They only had thirty minutes left. It was worth a shot. "We better hurry," he said, turning to Frank and Phil. "If we run, we can get to Fun World in ten minutes. This may be our only chance!"

⚛ 10 ⚛

The Race Is On!

When Joe, Frank, and Phil rounded the corner, they could see Mr. Roboto from nearly two blocks away. The late afternoon sun reflected off his silver body. He was standing right along the curb, music blasting from his ears. Someone had put a sign in his hands that read WELCOME TO FUN WORLD! He moved it up and down as the cars went past.

Some cars were stopped along Main Street. Other drivers beeped their horns or leaned out their windows. "Woo-hoo!" a kid hooted as his

mom sped away. He took off his green baseball hat

and waved it in the air. "Hi, Robot Man!"

"His name is Mr. Roboto!" Phil yelled. He sprinted toward the robot. He was so excited he wrapped his arms around the robot's sides, pretending to hug him. "You're alive! I'm so sorry!"

Joe laughed. "As alive as he ever was!"

Frank leaned down. He placed the remote-control car he'd been carrying right beside the other one. It was a little loose, but it fit in place. There were a few scratches here and there, and some paint was missing on his left side, but otherwise Mr. Roboto was fine. "He looks great," Frank said. "Do you think we can still make it?"

Joe scanned the Fun World parking lot. Every kid in Bayport knew about Fun World. Mr. Fun had been in charge of the arcade for years. There were rows and rows of video games, bumper cars, mechanical swings, and more. Every time Frank and Joe went, they stayed for hours.

Mr. Fun was walking out of the front entrance. He had a camera in his hand. "How do you like my new robot?" he called to them. "Can you believe someone was throwing this guy out? I guess what they say is true: One man's trash is another man's treasure! Why don't you pose with Robot Man?"

Mr. Fun held up the camera. He waved his hands for the boys to get together, but all three of them stood in place. "Mr. Fun, this is our robot. We made him for the school science fair," Frank explained.

"And they are almost done looking at all the projects," Joe said. He looked at his watch and frowned. "We need to get him to the school gymnasium before the judges leave."

Mr. Fun furrowed his brows. "What do you mean? This robot is yours?"

"We made him," Phil said. "I made a horrible

mistake and put him out by the trash last night."

"You don't say," Mr. Fun muttered. "I never would've taken him if I'd known he was someone's science fair project."

"We know it was an accident," Frank said.

Mr. Fun plucked the sign out of Mr. Roboto's hands. He pressed the buttons on Mr. Roboto's chest and the song ended. Mr. Roboto's arms stopped moving. A few people in passing cars beeped louder. A few kids with ice-cream cones paused on the sidewalk. "Hey! Why'd you do that?" a boy with braces yelled.

"Is there anything I can do?" Mr. Fun asked. He rubbed his forehead with his hand—something he always did when he was upset. "How can I help?"

Joe looked at his watch, then at Mr. Fun's red pickup truck. If they set Mr. Roboto flat on his back, he wouldn't get ruined on their drive back to school. "Can you take us to the science fair?" Joe asked. "We don't have much time until the judges leave."

"You got it!" Mr. Fun yelled. He was about to say something else, but the boys all ran to Mr. Roboto. Phil grabbed his arms. Joe and Frank pushed him forward. They moved like that, rolling the robot as fast as they could. After a whole day searching for their project, they'd finally found him. But was it already too late?

"Watch out!" Joe yelled. "Robot coming through!"

They raced through the crowd, weaving Mr. Roboto past little children and an old man with a cane. The gymnasium was packed. So many people had come for the science fair. Parents had brought their small children to see the different projects. Two blond girls stopped in front of Iola's hermit crabs, their noses pressed against the glass tank.

In one corner the soccer team was having

a bake sale to raise money. There was a whole table covered in brownies, cupcakes, and cookies. "Mmmmm . . . ," Joe said. He stared at the cookies, stopping for a second. Frank pulled him away.

"There's no time!" Frank yelled. They glanced at the clock on the wall. It read 4:47. Principal Butler was across the gymnasium. She stood beside the judges. All three judges were scribbling on their clipboards, looking very serious.

"Oh no . . . ," Joe said. "They've already started the scoring." They wheeled Mr. Roboto past Cissy's butterfly project and Ellie's giant poster.

"Wow!" Ellie cried out. "Is that your project?"

Frank and Joe couldn't help but smile. "It is! Meet Mr. Roboto!" Frank yelled. As they wheeled him through more people, the funniest thing happened. Everyone turned. Some of the kids standing by the bleachers smiled and waved at the giant robot. Others came closer to get a better look.

Mimi Morton, Chet and Iola's little sister, even started clapping. "That's the coolest thing I've ever seen!" she cried.

They pushed Mr. Roboto right up to the judges. "I'm afraid you're late, boys," Principal Butler said. She folded her arms over her chest as she looked at the clock. "We've already finished the judging."

"We got here as fast as we could," Joe explained. "There was a mix-up, and Mr. Fun saw our robot by the garbage cans outside Phil's house. He brought him to Fun World. It took us this long to find him!"

Principal Butler glanced at the judges. The woman with the gray streak in her hair was smiling.

Phil stepped forward, sensing that was his cue. "We all worked very hard on our project, and Joe and Frank spent days putting the finishing touches on. They said from the beginning he was the best robot they'd ever seen. I wish I had believed them."

Phil glanced sideways at the boys, offering them a small smile. Then he pushed a few of the buttons on Mr. Roboto's chest. Music blasted from Mr. Roboto's ears. His head began to spin. His arms moved up and down. "We used a motor from a blender to make his head spin. The radio for his head lets him play music." Phil pushed the flap at the top of Mr. Roboto's chest, revealing the wires inside. "All the machinery is right there if you'd like to take a look."

The woman moved in to inspect the robot. Meanwhile, Frank pulled the walkie-talkie out of his pocket. He hid behind Joe as he spoke into it. "I even talk!" he whispered.

The words sounded from the speaker in Mr. Roboto's chest. The judge was so surprised she jumped. "This is very impressive," she said. The other two judges nodded in agreement. Then they flipped a new sheet open and scribbled something down. Phil blushed so much his ears turned red.

Frank, Joe, and Phil stood back, waiting to hear what they'd say. A small crowd had formed around Mr. Roboto. Some people poked at his remote-control car feet. Others swayed to the music coming out of his ears. Whether the boys won or lost, one thing was certain: Everyone loved Mr. Roboto.

After fifteen minutes Principal Butler called out to the crowd. "All right! We have our winners to announce!" Phil was so nervous he couldn't stand still. He squeezed Joe's arm so hard it hurt. Cissy, Chet, Iola, and Ellie all gathered beside them, the rest of the entries behind them. "Third place goes to Ellie Freeman, for answering the question 'Why is the sky blue?'" Ellie's whole face turned red. She walked in front of the crowd, and the judges handed her a yellow ribbon.

"Maybe you were right—maybe we *do* have a

chance?" Phil whispered to Joe. "I just wish I'd believed that before."

"It doesn't matter either way," Frank said. "We never wanted to win the science fair; we just wanted to build a project with you."

Principal Butler stepped forward to announce the runner-up. Her eyes scanned the crowd. It was getting closer to the moment everyone had been waiting for. For weeks everyone at Bayport had

been working on their projects. Frank and Joe had spent two weekends planning the robot with Phil before they put the first pieces together. Phil clasped his hands together. "Everyone loved Iola's hermit crabs. If she won, I wouldn't be surprised. I didn't know how many times they changed shells."

"And the second-place ribbon goes to . . . ," Principal Butler said loudly. The crowd

was silent. She flipped through the clipboard. "Cissy Zermeño! She did an excellent project on the life cycle of the butterfly." Cissy smiled. Principal Butler handed her a red ribbon. She pinned it onto her shirt, wearing it proudly.

Principal Butler cleared her throat. She flipped to another page in the clipboard. She moved so slowly, the seconds passed like hours. "And first place goes to . . ." She looked around the room, adding a dramatic pause. "Phil Cohen, Frank Hardy, and Joe Hardy, for their robot."

"We did it!" Joe cried. The three boys went to the front of the crowd. Together, they accepted the blue first-place ribbon. Everyone clapped for them. Frank hadn't been so happy since the Bandits had won the Little League championship!

"I know who really deserves this," Phil said. He pressed the ribbon onto Mr. Roboto's chest. Mr. Roboto moved his arms up and down like he was dancing. The entire crowd cheered. It was official—their new friend was a huge hit!

Now there was only one thing left to do. . . .

After all the excitement of the day, Frank and Joe returned to their tree house. They had made an agreement with Phil. They would take Mr. Roboto for one week, and then Phil would have him at his house for the next. That way they were all able to play with the robot as much as possible. Now that the science fair was over, they could do what they did best—have fun!

Frank wrote *Secret Files Case #11* on the big whiteboard that hung on the wall. Then, right underneath it, he wrote *Solved!* Phil had kept apologizing, but Joe and Frank had told him it was okay. Everyone made mistakes. Besides, Mr. Fun had felt so bad about what had happened that he gave all three boys free passes to Fun World for the month. Now Phil, Joe, and Frank could all use the passes together.

"What do you think about that, Mr. Roboto?" Joe asked. He pressed the button on the robot's chest and music played. The robot's head spun around.

"That must mean he liked it!" Frank laughed.

Joe and Frank high-fived. Another Secret Files case: Solved!

FRANK AND JOE AREN'T SO SURE. . . .

Nancy Drew and the Clue Crew

Test your detective skills with more Clue Crew cases!

FROM ALADDIN • PUBLISHED BY SIMON & SCHUSTER

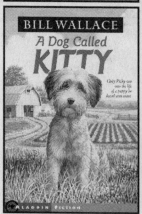

Join Zeus and his friends as they set off on the adventure of a lifetime.

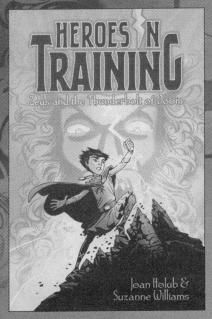

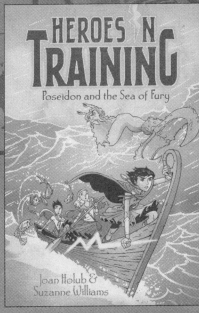